D0516365

Disney's
My Very First Winnie the Pooh ™

Safe in the Woods with Pooh

by

Barbara Gaines Winkelman

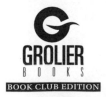

GROLIER
B O O K S
BOOK CLUB EDITION

Based on the Pooh stories by A. A. Milne
(copyright The Pooh Properties Trust).

Printed in the United States of America.

First published by Disney Press, New York, NY
This edition published by Grolier Books, ISBN: 0-7172-8927-3
Grolier Books is a division of Grolier Enterprises, Inc.

Tap, tap, tap . . . . Someone was knocking at Pooh's door.

"Wake up, Pooh," Piglet's voice squeaked from the other side of the door. "Today is the day Kanga is going to bake us a pie and have a special sunny-day party."

Pooh stretched happily. He could see the sunshine streaming in his window. Pooh quickly got dressed and, without stopping to take his nightcap off, he ran outside.

"Good morning, Piglet! What a day!" cried Pooh. "Let's go pick berries for Kanga's pie."

"That's just what I was thinking, Pooh," answered Piglet. "Where shall we go?"

"Perhaps we should follow our noses," suggested Pooh as they started off down the path.

"Oh, look . . . berries!" Pooh said after a while. "They look perfect for Kanga's pie!"

"W-well, do you know what these berries are, Pooh?" asked Piglet.

"No, but they look ripe and delicious!" replied Pooh. "We can use my nightcap as a bucket, see?" he added. Pooh picked a berry and was about to pop it into his mouth.

"Stop, Pooh!" Piglet cried. "Don't eat it!"

"Why not, Piglet?" asked Pooh, looking puzzled.

"Remember what Christopher Robin told us?" Piglet reminded Pooh. "'Don't eat anything you pick in the woods unless a grown-up says it is good for you to eat.'"

"Yes, I remember now," Pooh sighed. "Oh, bother!" Then he cheered up. "I may be a bear of very little brain, but I have an idea! Let's go ask Owl. His house is right over there in that big tree."

"Hello, Owl," Pooh said when Owl opened his door. "Would you tell us if some berries we found will make us sick?"

"Dear, dear," said Owl in a worried voice.

"The berries are right over there, Owl," Pooh showed him with a wave of his paw. "Piglet reminded me that we have to ask someone who knows. So, we came to you!"

Pooh gave Owl a big smile.

"Of course, of course!" said Owl. "Excellent thinking, Pooh! Let's have a look!" So the three of them went back to the berry patch.

"Ah, yes!" exclaimed Owl. "These blackberries will not harm anyone. They are perfectly edible and exceedingly delicious. As a matter of fact, I happen to know that Kanga will love these for the pie she is planning to bake today."

Pooh popped a berry in his mouth. Then he ate another and another.

"Pooh?" Piglet said gently, "perhaps we should stop eating the berries and start collecting some for Kanga's pie."

"Oh, that's a good idea, Piglet," chuckled Pooh, and he began to gather berries, using his nightcap as a bucket.

So they filled up Pooh's nightcap and carried the berries to Kanga.

As they passed Roo's sandy place, they met
Roo. He became so excited at all the berries
Pooh and Piglet had gathered that he ran ahead
to tell Kanga all about it.

Kanga was delighted with the berries. Soon she had a freshly baked pie for all the friends to share. It was delicious!

"Now is it time for fun and games, Mama?" asked Roo when everyone had finished.

"Tiggers like fun and games!" said Tigger. "Who wants to play in the woods with me?"

"I do! I do!" cried Roo. "Can I, Mama? Can I?"

"Yes, you may, dear," answered Kanga. "Just stay with Tigger."

"Yippee!" Tigger and Roo cheered together.

Meanwhile, Pooh and Piglet tried to decide what kind of fun *they* would have together.

"Do you know what, Piglet?" announced Pooh. "On a nice day like this, I'd like to go fishing in the stream."

"Oh, yes!" shouted Piglet with glee. "And I like *swimming* in the stream, so we could go together! You can be my buddy!"

"That's true, Piglet," said Pooh, "except . . . don't you remember the safe-in-the-woods rule that says you are not to swim while someone is fishing nearby?"

"Oh, you're right, Pooh. I do remember now," agreed Piglet.

Pooh and Piglet were silent for a moment, deep in thought. Then Pooh's face brightened.

"Piglet!" he said. "First, I'll be your buddy and sit on the bank and watch while you swim!"

"Yes! Then I'll stop swimming so you can go fishing, Pooh," Piglet cried, "and I will sit with you and keep you company while you fish."

"We'll take turns!" shouted Piglet and Pooh together.

So that is just what they did!

As Pooh and Piglet sat on the bank waiting for a fish to bite, they heard a noise, ". . .10 . . . 11 . . . 12 . . . "

It sounded like someone counting. Piglet and Pooh listened hard, ". . . 13 . . . 14 . . . 15 . . . 16 . . . ." It *was* someone counting!

"I th-think I know that voice," Piglet whispered. They listened some more, ". . . 17 . . . 18 . . . 19 . . . ."

"It's Tigger!" exclaimed Pooh.

Roo and Tigger were playing hide-and-seek nearby. Tigger was counting. Roo found a hollow log. It was cozy inside—a wonderful hiding place to wait for Tigger to find him! Roo crawled in and made himself comfortable.

"... **20!**" Tigger shouted. "Okay, Buddy Boy! Ready or not, here I come!"

Tigger searched for Roo. Then he searched some more. But he couldn't find him. So he searched even more, calling out over and over, "Roo, li'l buddy! I give up! Where are you?" But still no Roo.

Pooh and Piglet heard Tigger calling and calling, so they ran over to see if they could help. Just as they got there, Rabbit and Christopher Robin arrived, too.

"But, Tigger, why didn't you use the buddy rule?" asked Rabbit when he heard what was happening.

"What's the buddy rule?" Tigger asked.

"Roo is too young to be all by himself," explained Christopher Robin. "He should always have a buddy with him."

"But he had a buddy with him," said Tigger. "*I'm* his bestest buddy!"

"No, Tigger," said Christopher Robin. "Roo hid alone. He should have a buddy hiding with him."

"If Roo got stuck," Piglet squeaked excitedly, "his buddy could go get help for him."

"Oh, what have I done?" wailed Tigger. "I let my buddy down!"

"Don't worry, Tigger," said Christopher Robin. "We'll find Roo. Let's spread out and look for him."

Pooh and Piglet
went and looked in
Pooh's house.

Rabbit looked in the
sandy place.

Tigger scanned the
stream from a hill.
But no Roo.

Christopher Robin stayed by the tree where Tigger had counted. He looked around. "Where could little Roo be?" wondered Christopher Robin. His eyes settled on a hollow log. Kneeling down, he looked inside.

"Here he is, everybody!" Christopher Robin called out. "I found him!"

"Roo, li'l buddy!" yelled Tigger, bouncing up. "Thank goodness! I thought I losted you!"

Roo stretched and yawned. "I fell asleep," he said.

"You have to be careful, Roo," warned Christopher Robin. "You might have gotten stuck inside a log this narrow, and you had no buddy with you to go get help."

"This has certainly been a day for learning how to be safe in the woods!" chuckled Pooh.

"I know what," said Rabbit. "I am going to organize a list of safe-in-the-woods rules."

"Hooray!" shouted Tigger. "Roo and I wanna learn *all* the safe-woods rules. 'Cause from now on, we're gonna be good, careful buddies. Right, Roo?"

"Right!" squeaked Roo, happily bouncing with Tigger.

And here is the list Rabbit made:

Safe-in-the-Woods Rules:

- Do not eat anything you pick in the woods unless a grown-up tells you it is good to eat.

- Always have a buddy with you when you are playing in the woods.

- Always have a buddy with you when you go swimming.

- Do not fish where others are swimming.

- Do not swim where others are fishing.

- Do not hide in small, closed places where you could get stuck.